MW00930179

You Bee you, and I'll Bee me

Written by

Annick Patry

ISBN: 978-1-961028-49-4

Dedicated

to my granddaughter Blake.
The world seems complicated
but it doesn't have to bee!!

At first it was hard, I would see other bees flying and wondered why I couldn't fly.

I also found by doing so, I could collect more pollen by starting from the ground up.

After a while I understood who I was and that I could do everything a normal bee can do.

Everybody is this kind, they just need to let others be, dig deeper into their hearts and ignore all the buzzing around them.

You are so right!

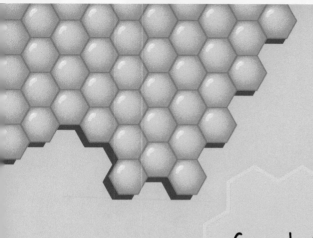

Can we be friends?

Of course we can be friends, let's spread the word of kindness together! Hop on I will lead the way!

to my dreariest Blake

Printed in the USA
CPSIA information can be obtained
at www.ICGtesting.com
LVHW072347261023
762144LV00012B/58